D1104995

A Note to Parents and Caregivers:

Read-it! Readers are for children who are just starting on the amazing road to reading. These beautiful books support both the acquisition of reading skills and the love of books.

 The PURPLE LEVEL presents basic topics and objects using high frequency words and simple language patterns.

 The RED LEVEL presents familiar topics using common words and repeating sentence patterns.

 The BLUE LEVEL presents new ideas using a larger vocabulary and varied sentence structure.

 The YELLOW LEVEL presents more challenging ideas, a broad vocabulary, and wide variety in sentence structure.

 The GREEN LEVEL presents more complex ideas, an extended vocabulary range, and expanded language structures.

 The ORANGE LEVEL presents a wide range of ideas and concepts using challenging vocabulary and complex language structures.

When sharing a book with your child, read in short stretches, pausing often to talk about the pictures. Have your child turn the pages and point to the pictures and familiar words. And be sure to reread favorite stories or parts of stories.

There is no right or wrong way to share books with children. Find time to read with your child, and pass on the legacy of literacy.

Adria F. Klein, Ph.D.
Professor Emeritus
California State University
San Bernardino, California

Editors: Christianne Jones and Dodie Marie Miller
Page Production: Brandie Shoemaker
Art Director: Nathan Gassman

First American edition published in 2007 by
Picture Window Books
5115 Excelsior Boulevard
Suite 232
Minneapolis, MN 55416
877-845-8392
www.picturewindowbooks.com

© Text copyright Martin Waddell 2003

This Americanization of CHARLIE'S TASKS was originally published in English
in 2003 under the title CHARLIE'S STORIES by arrangement with Oxford
University Press.

All rights reserved. No part of this book may be reproduced without written permission
from the publisher. The publisher takes no responsibility for the use of any of the
materials or methods described in this book, nor for the products thereof.

Printed in the United States of America.

Library of Congress Cataloging-in-Publication Data
Waddell, Martin.
Charlie's tasks / by Martin Waddell ; illustrated by Daniel Postgate.
p. cm. — (Read-it! readers)
Summary: Charlie always finds unorthodox ways of completing the tasks Farmer
Oldboots gives him to do, from getting mud out of the bottom of the well to driving
the wagon home from the fair.
ISBN-13: 978-1-4048-3137-7 (library binding)
ISBN-10: 1-4048-3137-1 (library binding)
[1. Work—Fiction. 2. Helpfulness—Fiction.] I. Postgate, Daniel, ill. II. Title.
PZ7.W1137Cha 2006
[E]—dc22   2006029120

Charlie's Tasks

by Martin Waddell
illustrated by Daniel Postgate

Special thanks to our advisers for their expertise:

Adria F. Klein, Ph.D.
Professor Emeritus, California State University
San Bernardino, California

Susan Kesselring, M.A.
Literacy Educator
Rosemount–Apple Valley–Eagan (Minnesota) School District

CONNETQUOT PUBLIC LIBRARY
760 OCEAN AVENUE
BOHEMIA, NEW YORK 11716
Tel: (631) 567-5079

Every day Farmer Oldboots had a morning task and an afternoon task for Charlie.

Charlie usually messed up the tasks, but the farmer kept trying. Because Charlie was a nice guy, the farmer didn't fire him.

For his morning task one day, Farmer Oldboots called Charlie out to the old well.

"What do you see in the well, Charlie?" asked the farmer.

"I see me," Charlie said, sounding surprised.

"What else do you see?" Farmer Oldboots asked patiently.

"Well water!" said Charlie.

"There's more mud down there than well water," said Farmer Oldboots.

"Right!" Charlie said.

"I want all that mud out of this well!" said Farmer Oldboots. "See to it, Charlie!"

The farmer went off to his house. Ned came along. He saw Charlie standing by the old well. Charlie scratched his head and looked puzzled. "What's up, Charlie?" asked Ned.

"Farmer Oldboots wants the mud out of the well," Charlie said slowly. "But how can we get the mud out of the well?"

"I know!" said Ned. "We'll get buckets and lower them into the well. Then we can get the mud out."

So Ned fetched buckets, and they got the
mud out. Soon there were buckets and buckets
of mud all around the well.

Charlie looked at the buckets of mud. He
scratched his head and looked puzzled.

"What's up, Charlie?" asked Ned.

"What should we do with the mud in the buckets?" Charlie asked.

"We better ask Sid," Ned said. "He'll know what to do."

When Sid arrived, he looked at the mud in the buckets.

"I know!" Sid said. "We'll get shovels and dig a big hole. When the hole's dug, we can put the mud in it."

So they dug a big hole beside the well. It took a long time and a whole lot of digging. Then they poured the mud into the hole they had dug. Charlie, Ned, and Sid patted it down with their shovels so the field would be flat.

"Job well done, Charlie!" gasped Ned and Sid.

Charlie looked at the big pile of dirt they had dug from the hole by the well. Charlie scratched his head and looked puzzled.

"What's up, Charlie?" said Sid.

"What should we do with the big pile of dirt?" Charlie said.

Ned and Sid thought for a bit.

"We better ask Bert!" said Ned and Sid. "He'll know what to do."

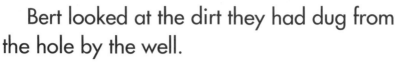

Bert looked at the dirt they had dug from the hole by the well.

"I know," Bert said. "We'll shovel the earth down the old well!"

"Great idea, Bert!" they all said.

"I'm happy to be done with one task," Charlie said.

Charlie took a break, ate lunch, and reported back to Farmer Oldboots.

"My morning task is done, boss,"
Charlie said.

"It's about time," Farmer Oldboots
said. "Now you can do your afternoon task,
which is to take me to the market."

At the market, the farmer bought a cow, a pig, and a chicken. Then he climbed up on the cart and lay down.

"Home, Charlie!" yawned Farmer Oldboots. "If you value your job, don't wake me up until we're there!"

Charlie looked at Horse Herbert, his friend, who was pulling the cart.

"Neigh!" Horse Herbert said, shaking his head. In horse talk this means, "I can't pull that load in my cart."

"What can we do?" Charlie thought.

"Follow us home, behind the cart," Charlie told the cow, the pig, and the chicken.

Charlie climbed on the cart, and they set off for home. The cow, the pig, and the chicken walked behind the cart that Horse Herbert was pulling.

The chicken's short legs soon got tired.
So Charlie put the chicken on top of the pig.
The chicken rode on the pig's back, behind the
cow and the cart that Horse Herbert was pulling.

Then the pig got tired. So Charlie put the pig and the chicken on top of the cow. They set off again, with the pig and chicken riding the cow, behind the cart that Horse Herbert was pulling.

But it was all too much for the cow. Charlie loaded them all into the cart.

21

"Be careful!" he warned them. "Don't wake up Farmer Oldboots."

When Horse Herbert tried to move, he fell over. There was too much weight in the cart.

"Neigh!" Horse Herbert said, twitching his tail. In horse talk this means, "I can't do it!"

"What can we do?" Charlie thought.

They both stood and thought for a bit.

"Neigh Neigh Neigh!" Horse Herbert said, pricking up his ears. In horse talk this means, "Why not ask Farmer Oldboots?"

"I'm not waking up Farmer Oldboots!" Charlie said.

So they thought a bit more.

"You pull. I'll get behind and push the cart!"
Charlie said to Horse Herbert.
　　But that meant no one was driving the cart.
So the cart ended up in the ditch.
　　"What can we do?" Charlie thought.

"I can't push and steer!" Charlie said.
"I'll have to find someone to do it!"
    The best someone was Farmer Oldboots.
But Charlie knew he couldn't wake him up.

"I need someone to steer!" Charlie said to the cow, the pig, and the chicken. "Who will volunteer?"

"Cluck!" said the chicken. In chicken talk this means, "Chickens don't steer."

"Oink!" said the pig. In pig talk this means, "Not this pig."

"Moo! Moo! Moo!" sighed the cow. In cow talk this means, "I'll try."

It was very brave of the cow.

The cow took the reins of the cart. But cows don't steer carts often. They wound up in the ditch again.

"Oh, dear!" Charlie said. "Horse Herbert, what can we do?"

They both stood and thought a bit more. "Neigh! Neigh! Neigh!" Horse Herbert sighed. In horse talk this means, "I suppose I could do it."

Charlie went to the front where Horse Herbert had been, and Horse Herbert climbed up on the cart.

Horse Herbert picked up the reins and drove the cart back to the farm without waking up Farmer Oldboots.

Like always, Charlie completed both of his tasks. He couldn't wait to show the farmer the well and tell him how they got back to the farm. He knew Farmer Oldboots would be pleased with his work. Why else would he keep giving him tasks?

More *Read-it!* Readers

Bright pictures and fun stories help you practice your reading skills. Look for more books at your level.

Alex and Toolie

Another Pet

The Big Pig

Bliss, Blueberries, and the Butterfly

Camden's Game

Cass the Monkey

Clever Cat

Flora McQuack

Kyle's Recess

Marconi the Wizard

Peppy, Patch, and the Postman

Peter's Secret

Pets on Vacation

The Princess and the Tower

Theodore the Millipede

The Three Princesses

Tromso the Troll

Willie the Whale

The Zoo Band

Looking for a specific title or level? A complete list of *Read-it!* Readers is available on our Web site: **www.picturewindowbooks.com**

AUG   2007

CONNETQUOT PUBLIC LIBRARY

0621 9100 432 190 4

$ 19.93

CONNETQUOT PUBLIC LIBRARY
760 Ocean Avenue
Bohemia, NY   11716
631-567-5079

Library Hours:

Monday-Friday	**9:00 - 9:00**
Saturday	**9:00 - 5:00**
Sunday (Oct.-May)	**1:00 - 5:00**

GAYLORD M